D1146197

characters created by
lauren child

Boo!
MADE you
jump!

PUFFIN

Text based on the script written by Dave Ingham

Illustrations from the TV animation

produced by Tiger Aspect

PUFFIN BOOKS
Published by the Penguin Group: London, New York, Australia,
Canada, India, Ireland, New Zealand and South Africa
Penguin Books Ltd, Registered Offices: 80 Strand, London WC2R 0RL, England

puffinbooks.com

This edition published in Great Britain in Puffin Books 2012
001 – 10 9 8 7 6 5 4 3 2 1
Text and illustrations copyright © Lauren Child/Tiger Aspect Productions Limited, 2008
Charlie and Lola word and logo ® and © Lauren Child, 2005
Charlie and Lola is produced by Tiger Aspect Productions
All rights reserved
The moral right of the author/illustrator has been asserted
Manufactured in China
ISBN: 978-0-718-19529-8
This edition produced for the Book People Ltd,
Hall Wood Avenue, Haydock, St Helens, WA11 9UL

I have this little sister Lola.
She is small and very funny.
I am always making her jump...

But she can **NEVER** make me jump.

Lola says,
"But I really want to make
you jump, Charlie."

And I say,
"OK, Lola, but that will
NEVER happen."

In the park,
Lola and Lotta scream,

"Boo!"

Lola says, "You **jumped**, Charlie. I saw you."

And I say,
"Don't be silly, Lola.
You'll never make **ME** jump."

Later, Lola and Lotta
        try to **scare** me and Marv
while we watch TV.

"Oooooohhh... " "Oooooohhhh.. "

So I say, "Hi, Lola."

And Marv says, "Hi, Lotta."

That night, Lola says,
"I'm going to tell you a really scary
story about a terribly
terrible, very old castle full
of icky sticky spiders."

So I say,
"Oh, this story won't make anyone **jump**."

But Lola says,
"Yes it WILL, Charlie...

"Once upon a time, there were two boys and two not-quite-so-biggish
small girls. And they were lost.

They were SO lost that they
went up to a spooky castle
to ask the way.

"They opened the door of the **scary** castle
and went up the **creaky** stairs."

Then Lotta asks, "Do we have to go up there?"
"Yes," says Lola.
"That's what you do in **scary** stories...

And, as they followed the biggest boy
up the **creaky** stairs, they heard—"

"A **ghost**!" shouts Marv.
"I'm scared," says Lotta.
"I'm NOT," I say.

"Anyway, at the very, very top of the stairs,"
says Lola, "there was another
great big, ENORMOUS
door.

And, as the boy, who looked a bit like Charlie, turned the handle, the ghosty sound got louder and LOUDER... And do you know who it was?" asks Lola.

"Meow"

"It was Twinkle!
	Mrs Elmore's kitten
from next door."

"Oh, Lola!" I say.

"How is a little furry animal
going to make anyone jump?"

But just then...

"AHHHHH!" I shout.

"SIZZLES, you really made me **jump**."

"Hmmm," says Lola.
    "Now I know how to
make you jump, Charlie."

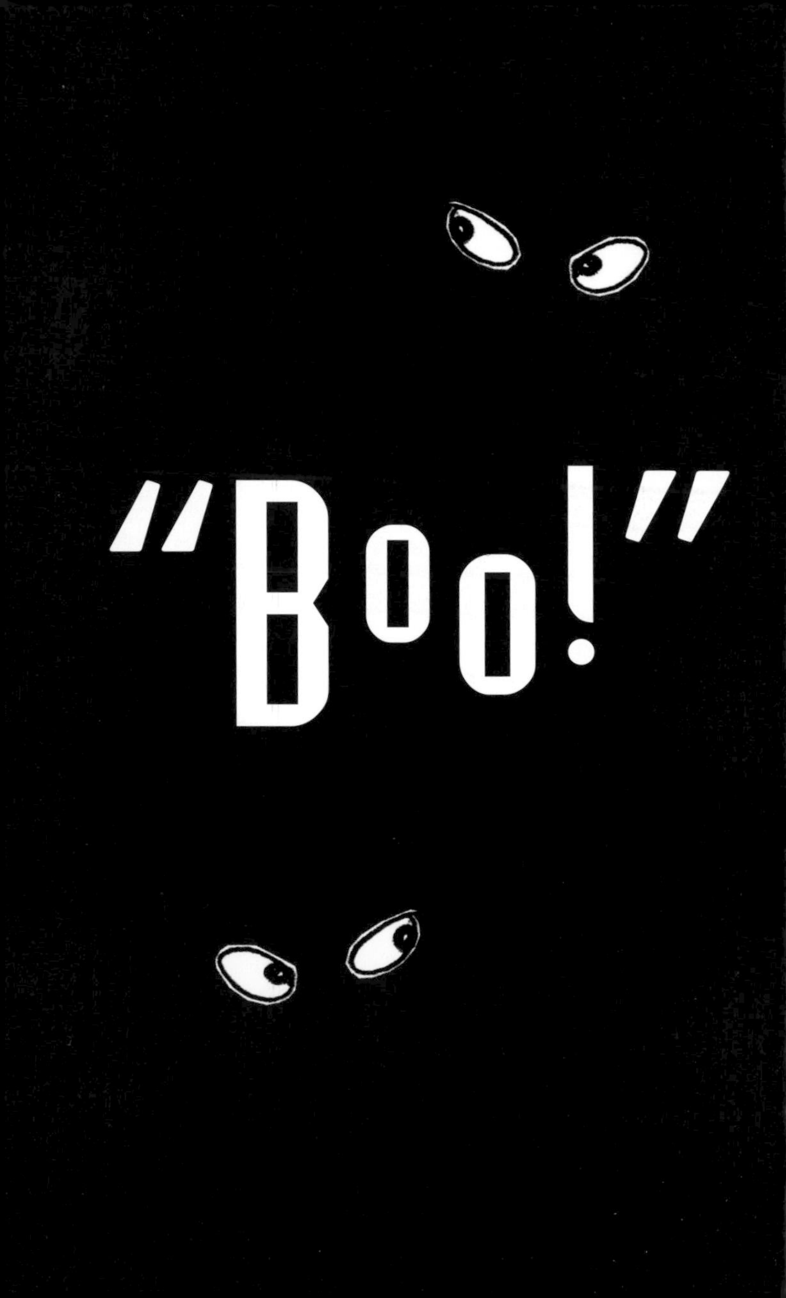
"Boo!"